MW01104345

ROCKHOUND
SCIENCE
MYSTERIES

By Mark H. Newhouse

Illustrations by Denise Gilgannon

Executive Producer . . . . Carol Stern
Producer . . . . Denise Welborn
Layout Design . . . . Stacy Miller

© MCMXCIX

ISBN 978-0-9704629-4-7

www.earthkidspublishing.com

ROCKHOUND FILES: ROCKHOUND'S JUICIEST CASE

Rockhound the detective heard someone tapping at his door. When he opened the door, he was surprised to see ... two wide-eyed pups!

"Hello! I'm Crystal. My brother is Chip. We need a detective."

Rockhound was not used to such young clients.

"What's the problem?" asked Rockhound.

"We're being cheated, but we can't prove it!" Crystal said. "It began when we got that new cafeteria lady, Myrtle. Our other cafeteria ladies were really great, and our lunches were delicious, but now the food Myrtle gives us is terrible."

"Yeah, it's awful! Especially the juice," Chip interrupted. "Yuck!"

"We think she's adding a lot of water to it," explained Crystal. "She charges us for pure juice and keeps the extra money."

"She says we're just puppies and we don't know nothing," Chip yelped.

"Anything, Chip. Anything! How many times do I have to correct you?" complained Crystal.

Chip growled, "Anything! Okay?"

Rockhound sighed, "This doesn't sound like a case for a detective. Did you tell your parents?"

"They don't believe us. We have no proof," Crystal replied. "We thought a detective could prove we're right."

"How?" Rockhound asked. "By tasting the juice? I don't see how we can prove that the juice is being monkeyed with. I'm really sorry."

"Let's get going, Chip," Crystal muttered. "He won't help us."

Chip followed along with his sister. "Good-bye, Mr. Detective," he said. "Thank you for listening anyway."

"Dog biscuits!" Rockhound grumbled. "If only there were a way I

4

could help them."

Rockhound decided to visit the Canine School.

At the school, Rockhound followed the scent of kibble until he came to the cafeteria. It looked dark. He thought he was all alone, but suddenly he heard a voice.

He crept inside to take a closer look. He saw a gigantic dog talking on the telephone. She looked like a ghost.

"I think those bratty pups are getting wise to me. I'd better be more careful." Her voice became icy. "I tell you now, nobody better get in my way. Nobody!" Suddenly she whirled toward the door. "I think I heard something!"

She threw the door open and called out, "Is someone there?"

Rockhound jumped under a

table. If that cafeteria creature found him, there would be no telling what might end up in the school lunch the next day!

He held his breath until he heard her speaking on the phone again. Whew! Rockhound's breath rushed out of his lungs.

Rockhound hurried to his car. As he drove away, he tried to think of a way to trap Myrtle.

Suddenly he spotted Crystal. She was licking an ice pop, not missing a drop. Nearby, Chip was slobbering the sticky liquid all over his chin.

"Isn't he a pig?" Crystal teased. "Look at that mess!"

Chip stopped slobbering long enough to make a face at her.

"He's enjoying himself," Rockhound laughed. He explained that he was working on their case, but still couldn't think of a way to prove that the cafeteria juice wasn't pure.

"Taste it," Chip suggested.

"We need scientific proof," explained Rockhound.

"Don't worry," Chip snorted. "You'll figure out something. I've got confidence in you."

Rockhound quietly watched Chip struggling with his ice pop. Suddenly Rockhound gasped. "It's simple! You've given me the answer!"

"Me?" Chip asked, juice trickling down his chin.

"Yes," Rockhound howled, "you and your sticky ice pop have solved the mystery! Why didn't I think of it before?"

"Think of what?" Chip asked.

"A test to prove your juice isn't pure! If I'm right, that cafeteria lady will soon be 'on ice' herself!"

STUDENT PREDICTION PAGE:
What do you think the outcome will be?
Write your prediction on these pages.

_____

_____

_____

_____

_____

_____

_____

_____

9

AND NOW BACK TO OUR STORY...

Rockhound bought a container of pure orange juice and headed back to the school. It was time to confront the conniving cafeteria lady!

"I'd like to perform an experiment for the students," Rockhound explained to Myrtle, the cafeteria lady. "I'm going to make ice pops for the pups."

"How nice," Myrtle wheezed.

Rockhound said, "I'll need some orange juice . . ."

Myrtle grumbled, but got the juice. Rockhound poured it into some paper cups and placed sticks in the cups.

"Oh," Rockhound said, "I forgot one thing. I've brought some of my own orange juice with me." He smiled at her as he poured the juice

into cups and labeled them "100% juice."

Myrtle wondered why he had brought his own juice.

"There," Rockhound announced. "We're ready for the freezer. You know, it amazes me how different liquids freeze at different rates of speed."

Myrtle was suddenly nervous.

"Yessiree," Rockhound chatted, "all this juice should freeze at the same time."

Myrtle was sweating. Her heart was pounding. This dog knew! He was trying to trap her!

Myrtle blurted out, "I have work to do, Mister . . . what did you say your name was?"

"Rockhound," he smiled. "Rockhound the detective."

Myrtle was startled. "Did you say

'detective'?"

Rockhound nodded. Myrtle worked nervously while Rockhound sat calmly waiting. Then Rockhound announced, "It's time to check the cups to see if they're frozen."

Rockhound looked at the cups. "I wonder why that happened! All of your juices are frozen . . . but not the pure orange juice."

Myrtle didn't wait for anything else. She screamed, throwing the tray of juice cups on Rockhound. She ran out of the door with Rockhound holding on.

Suddenly she slammed to a stop and Rockhound fell to the ground. "Let go of me!" she bellowed.

Just then, Myrtle noticed the hallway was clogged with every puppy in the school. She roared, "Get out of my way you brats!"

The puppies refused to move. Suddenly Chip, his voice trembling, said, "You're under arrest, cafeteria lady. Rockhound has proven you water down our orange juice. You won't be cheating us anymore."

"I'll bite your ears off," Myrtle growled, showing her teeth.

"I don't think so," Rockhound said, slapping handcuffs on her wrists. "I think your days of bullying these pups are over."

Myrtle collapsed like an emptied bag of flour.

"Well, pups," Rockhound said when it was all over, "I guess this case is closed."

"Yeah," Chip laughed. "You could say it was a tough squeeze."

Crystal playfully swatted Chip across his head while Rockhound laughed.

THE END

15

ROCKHOUND FILES:
THE FIZZLING
FOSSIL PUZZLER

The Weasel Mansion looked dark
and unfriendly. It was protected by
high, spiked fences and electrified
barbed wire.

Rockhound the detective held his identification card up to a security camera by the gate. The gate opened and he walked toward a huge steel door. Suddenly, it opened.

"We must be very careful," W.W. Weasel hissed as he opened the door and led Rockhound down a long hallway to a small, windowless room. A security camera was watching them from a corner of the ceiling.

"I need your help," Weasel whined. "They are trying to steal the DOGOSAURUS!"

So that's it, Rockhound thought. The Dogosaurus! The most valuable fossil in dog history!

"They'll stop at nothing to steal my treasure," Weasel continued.

Rockhound listened as Weasel related the long, involved history of the Dogosaurus Fossil, discovered

18

accidentally while digging up volcanic rock in Catsylvania.

Rockhound suddenly remembered. The Catsylvanians wanted the fossil back, but Weasel had refused. Now they were in court, fighting over who should own the precious relic.

"The Cats are trying to steal it," Weasel said, staring into Rockhound's face. "You must protect it."

"Why don't you call the police or the FBI? This sounds like a job for them," explained Rockhound.

"By the time they help, it will be too late," Weasel answered. "You are my only hope."

"I don't know," Rockhound answered. Something about this case was fishy.

Weasel smiled, "Even if you could help just until other arrangements are made."

Rockhound didn't like Weasel's smile. "Why in the world would the Catsylvanians steal what they'll probably win in court?" he asked.

Weasel snarled, "They won't win! The Dogosaurus is mine! Mine!" Rockhound jumped out of his seat.

Weasel calmed down. "Will you help me?"

"Show me the fossil," Rockhound said, not sure that he wanted to get involved.

"Impossible," Weasel declared. "Security reasons. You understand."

"I'm sorry," Rockhound said, moving toward the door, "I can't guard what I can't see."

"Wait. Please wait." Weasel circled behind Rockhound. "Be reasonable."

Rockhound was losing patience. "Call the FBI," he grunted.

"No!" Weasel shouted. "I want you! With you, I know the fossil will be safe."

Rockhound liked compliments, but not this time. "Do I see the fossil or not?" he demanded.

Weasel grumbled, "Very well. I will fetch it."

Rockhound didn't trust this character . . . something was definitely wrong. Suddenly he thought of a plan. "Where can I get some tea?" he asked, trying to sound friendlier.

Weasel looked surprised. "How thoughtless of me," he murmured. "What would you like?"

Rockhound smiled and requested, "Tea and fresh lemon please."

His host nodded and left the room.

Rockhound got ready.

Soon, Weasel returned with a

silver tray carrying tea and several slices of lemon. "I'll be back in a minute," Weasel muttered as he left the room to fetch the rare fossil.

Alone again, Rockhound turned his back to the video camera. He quickly placed a lemon slice into his coat pocket. He now had a way to test his suspicions. He sipped a little of the tea and made a face. Tea always tasted bitter to him.

"Here it is," Weasel announced, hugging a small wood box. "The famous Dogosaurus Fossil."

Weasel shoved the tea tray out the door, his eyes never leaving the locked box. He unlocked the box and gently placed the fossil on a clean cloth on the table.

Rockhound tried to hide his amazement. It was hard to believe that an object barely six inches long

24

could be of such value.

"To the uneducated, such as yourself," Weasel announced, "it looks worthless . . . like a common stone found in any backyard, not the remains of some prehistoric canine trapped in a volcanic flow. It's priceless!"

Rockhound moved to touch the fossil.

"No," Weasel growled. "Don't touch!"

"Give me a break," Rockhound barked. "I've got to examine this thing before I agree to protect it."

"Do be careful," Weasel reluctantly agreed. "It is priceless."

"Don't worry," Rockhound said. "I'll be gentle."

Rockhound reached to touch the stone. "Oh," he said suddenly.

"Something wrong?" Weasel was

alarmed.

Rockhound smiled, "It's nothing. My hands are sticky . . . from the tea. Have you a towel?"

Weasel looked annoyed. "I'll get something," he grumbled. "Wait here!"

Weasel scurried out muttering.

Rockhound quickly grabbed the lemon from his pocket and squeezed several drops over the fossil. . . . He stared down at the stone. Slowly, he smiled. His suspicions had been correct.

27

STUDENT PREDICTION PAGE:
What do you think the outcome will be?
Write your prediction on these pages.

_____

_____

_____

_____

_____

_____

_____

_____

AND NOW BACK TO OUR STORY...

In the dimly lit room, Rockhound had to bend down close to the fossil to be sure. The lemon juice was bubbling on the surface of the fossil. His hunch had been correct. He quickly tried it again. It was definitely fizzing. He quickly rubbed the lemon juice with his finger until the juice was invisible. Suddenly, the door opened with explosive speed. "Here," Weasel gasped, holding a paper towel.

Rockhound wiped his paws. He then bent closer, pretending to examine the fossil.

"Thank you," he said after several minutes, "I've seen enough."

Weasel watched Rockhound's every move. "You are satisfied?" he asked, locking away the Dogosaurus.

Rockhound smiled. "Oh, yes, I'm

31

completely satisfied."

"Good," Weasel said, rushing Rockhound outside. "You will begin now?"

"I need to get some help," Rockhound said, "then we'll be set."

"Good," Weasel said, a sly look on his face. "I feel much better."

"So do I," Rockhound replied, walking toward his car to phone the police.

The police arrested Weasel for stealing and selling the real Dogosaurus.

"But how did you know?" Weasel yelped.

"Detective secret," Rockhound said as they took Weasel away.

"How did you know?" his friend Captain Chihuahua asked. "This fossil looks real to me."

Rockhound explained he had been suspicious from the first. He couldn't understand why Weasel needed a detective. The FBI or Police would have done the job, and for free. "I figured he was pulling a fast one."

"What was his plan?" Captain Chihuahua asked.

"Well, the only thing that made sense," Rockhound continued, "was that Weasel had stolen the real Dogosaurus and sold it.

"I guessed that he wanted to convince the Catsylvanians that the fossil they would win in court was the true Dogosaurus. Weasel figured they wouldn't question it if he actually paid to have it protected. He just didn't count on me figuring out it was phony!"

"That was a good guess," Captain Chihuahua said, "but how did you know you were right?"

"I was lucky," Rockhound admitted. "I couldn't have been sure if I hadn't remembered that the genuine fossil was made of VOLCANIC rock. There was LIMESTONE in the fake."

"But how did you know that?" Chihuahua was puzzled.

"It was the bubbles," Rockhound explained. "I remembered from my elementary school science classes that when you drop lemon juice on limestone, it bubbles. Volcanic rock wouldn't have fizzed like that. Try it yourself with lemon juice or vinegar. If it hadn't had limestone in it, I would have had to try some other tests."

The Captain laughed, "You mean it really was 'elementary' this time?"

"I guess it was," Rockhound laughed. "You might say Wily Weasel's fossil fizzled!"

THE  END

35

ROCKHOUND FILES: JACK AND THE GREENSTALKS

Rockhound the detective stared at his host. The small reddish squirrel was seated on a chair in the center of a room whose floor was completely covered by a thin layer of white flour.

36

"I don't understand how they're doing it," his host muttered through clenched teeth. "I have taken every precaution I can think of . . . and they're still dying. It must be ghosts."

Rockhound had seen for himself the incredible alarm systems and the electronic gates that protected the house. Only a ghost could break into this house, he thought.

"Night and day, I stand guard. Every day I check the floor for footprints. Nothing! Absolutely nothing! And yet they're dying! Someone is killing them." The squirrel looked nervously around the room.

Rockhound found himself glancing nervously around the room as well. "Jack," he said in a calm voice, "who is dying?"

Jack looked up with large redlined eyes. "My precious babies. My wife left me to protect them while she takes care of her sick mother." He looked like he was about to cry. "I've tried everything, and I've failed."

"Babies!" Rockhound gasped. This was serious. "Where are these babies now?" Rockhound asked his host.

Jack stood up slowly. "Come with me," he said. "I'll show you." He led Rockhound toward the far wall of the room and shut off yet another alarm. He slid away a wall panel to reveal the huge steel door of a vault.

Rockhound gasped, "You keep your babies in a safe?"

"I just wanted to protect my wife's babies."

Rockhound glared at his host. "Whoever heard of keeping babies in a safe?" he growled as Jack turned the combination and pulled the handle. Jack guided him inside. "It's dark in here," Rockhound muttered.

Jack flicked on the lights.

"So where are these babies of yours?" Rockhound asked, angry that anyone would keep babies in a dark and airless safe.

"Here they are . . . my precious ones," Jack said as he pointed to a shelf at the back of the safe.

"They're . . . plants!" Rockhound shouted. "Your 'babies' are plants?"

The squirrel nodded his head. "They are my wife's most precious possessions. They're extremely rare and very expensive. She'll kill me when she sees them."

Rockhound examined the plants. They were indeed dying.

"How could anyone get near them?" the squirrel kept asking. "Do

you think it's poison?"

Rockhound was thinking. It didn't seem possible that anyone could bypass all of Jack Squirrel's alarms and poison his "babies," and yet, the plants were definitely dying. He stepped back out of the vault and stared at the flour-covered floor. "No footprints ever?" he asked Jack who was resealing the dark safe.

"None," Jack whined. "I tell you it's ghosts!"

"Ghosts," Rockhound said softly. "I don't think so."

"Then who?" Jack Squirrel asked. "Who is killing my plants?"

STUDENT PREDICTION PAGE:
What do you think the outcome will be?
Write your prediction on these pages.

_____

_____

_____

_____

_____

_____

_____

_____

_____

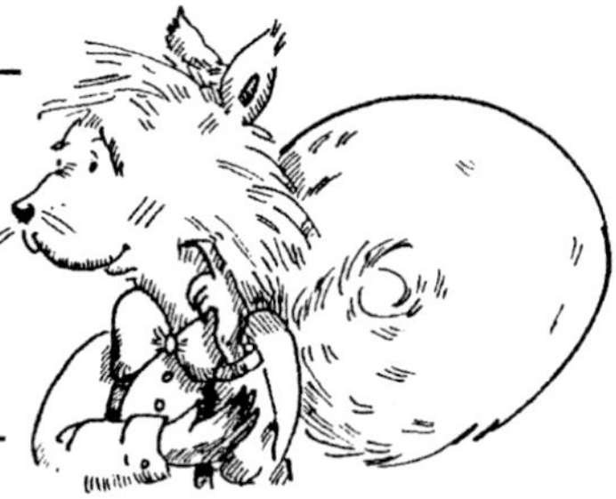

AND NOW BACK TO OUR STORY...

Rockhound looked at the squirrel with sympathetic eyes. "I think someone is killing your plants . . . I think it's you."

"Are you crazy?" the squirrel began to scream. "Me! I'd never do anything to hurt my babies!"

Rockhound sighed, "But you did. In trying to protect your plants, you almost killed them."

"How?" the upset squirrel cried out. "I wouldn't harm a hair on their little green leaves!"

Rockhound smiled, "Plants need sunlight and air to grow. You locked them in a dark and airless vault. Without air and light, your plants began to die."

The squirrel's mouth dropped open. "Air and light . . . You mean I was killing my own plants?"

Rockhound smiled, "You didn't mean to. Take them out of the safe and I think they'll be just fine."

Jack Squirrel grabbed Rockhound's paw. "Thank you! Thank you! How can I ever repay you?"

Rockhound smiled and said, "Just name one of the babies after me."

In a year's time, a beautiful Rock garden was thriving at Jack's house. It was filled with a variety of plants like Dog's-tooth Violets, Paw-paws, Horehound and Dog Fennel and was shaded by graceful Dogwood trees.

THE END